UNTHINKABLE

SHIRLEY DUKE

NIGHT FALL

UNTHINKABLE

SHIRLEY DUKE

MINNEAPOLIS

Darby Creek
A division of Lerner Publishing Group, Inc.
241 First Avenue North
Minneapolis, MN 55401 USA

For reading levels and more information, look up this title at www.lernerbooks.com.

Cover design: Emily Love
Cover photograph: Hannah Halkouskaya/iStockphoto; iStockphoto

Duke, Shirley Smith.
Unthinkable / by Shirley Duke.
p.   cm. — (Night fall)
ISBN 978-0-7613-6142-8 (lib. bdg. : alk. paper)
ISBN 978-0-7613-6545-7 (eb pdf)
[1. Horror stories.] I. Title.
PZ7.D88944Un   2010
[Fic]—dc22   2010003062

Manufactured in the United States of America
3-42914-11470-9/12/2016

To my parents,
Katie & G. L. Smith

Deep into that darkness peering, long I stood there wondering, fearing,
Doubting, dreaming dreams no mortal ever dared to dream before

—*Edgar Allan Poe,* The Raven

Omar Phillips
"Dead in Red"
Thursday, November 4, 2010, at 11:27 P.M.

*"Date from hell." If I live through this night, that's
how I'll remember it. If I don't, it's the end of my
remembering forever.*

*"I should have listened to you, Mom." That's what
I'll say, if I get the chance. I'll apologize too. Anything
to erase those last words to you tonight, that "I hate
you." You were right. Rick is a creep. More than a
creep. A psychopath. I got dressed up in my flame-red*

stiletto boots for a thirty-year-old serial killer I met on Facebook.

Oh, God! I can't quiet my breathing—and my heart. My body is like a loudspeaker, screaming, "Here I am. Come get me." He's stopped calling my name, but I can hear the branches snapping under his feet. It's like that game we used to play when we were kids. Cold, cold, warmer, warmer . . .

Hot! I can smell his cologne now, or maybe the sticky scent just won't stop gagging me from before.

"I didn't want to get in that car, Mom." That's what I'll tell you, if I ever get the chance. But his arm was squeezing my windpipe. I couldn't even breathe, much less fight.

But then I got away at the woods. Lunged for the car keys and went straight for the eyeballs. Felt the blood trickle onto my knuckles. Then I just ran like hell. And so here I am, in the shadow of a giant boulder. Here I am, scared out of my living mind, afraid to run cuz he'll hear my footsteps. Afraid to stay, gasping for air like a half-dead fish.

Hotter, hotter . . .

"Help! Heeeeelp me!"

I'm trying, Mom. Screaming my head off, kicking with my heels pointed out.

"Help me, someone! HELP ME!"

He's got me by the hair. I'm swatting, but my arms can't reach. Digging my heels into the ground.

He's dragging me now. Branches ripping my jeans and scratching my legs, my arms, stinging all over. Above, the moon a screaming white circle. Gnarled black branches reaching down for me.

We're stopping now. The ground feels soft. I can hear the water lapping on the shore. We're at the beach—his killing place.

It's no use. He's gonna kill me. Just like he killed the others. Untie my hair. Slice my neck. Tomorrow, you'll see me out there in the lake, my hair pooling around my head, face down, my feet—my red boots—bobbing slightly in the ripples.

This is it, Mom. He's untying my hair. Oh God, his fingers are on my neck. I'm sorry—

Omar read over his story. He'd written it so fast, fingers flying over the keys. He'd barely known what words he was putting down. All he knew was that the whole story had come over him like a nightmare, a waking nightmare. He'd *been* there, in the woods.

He'd heard the branches snapping, seen the killer's knife glinting in the moonlight. He'd smelled musky cologne and blood.

In a panic, Omar had turned to the one thing that always made him feel better—writing. Writing had made the vision go away. It had stilled his shaking hands and queasy stomach. Writing had made Omar feel calm—but not safe. *Something was wrong.*

T he next morning, Omar dragged himself out of bed. It had been a rotten night's sleep. It wasn't just the vision, either. Gabriel's screams had been especially piercing last night.

Gabriel was Omar's two-year-old brother. He suffered from what his mom called "night terrors." Gabriel would be fast asleep. Then, in one instant, he'd be sitting up, screaming his brains out. Lately Omar wondered if he had acquired his own brand of the same affliction.

Sometimes, when his mom was just too tired to deal, Omar would be the one to pick up Gabriel and hold him in a tight hug. It was terrifying to feel Gabriel's heart pounding against his own chest.

And the whole thing made Omar mad too. Gabriel had been a normal kid until their dad left. Gabriel's night terrors were the result of his "generalized anxiety" about that particular family situation. At least that's what the pediatrician had said. In Gabriel's two-year-old view, their dad had just magically disappeared—and that wasn't too far from the truth.

When Omar had asked why his dad was gone, his mom had given him some explanation about how it wasn't his fault and how much their dad still loved him and Gabriel. But on the night their dad left, Omar had heard him tell his mom that he felt "smothered." He needed "fresh air." That was ten months ago.

Since then, Omar's mom was either working or worrying about Gabriel. She spent her days getting cussed at or rolling her eyes about the customers at Lorraine's Eatery, off Highway 41. She spent her nights up with Gabriel. As for Omar, he was on his own. He could be a serial killer and she wouldn't notice.

This morning, the house was silent. Finally. Gabriel usually quieted down right about dawn. Then he and their mom slept like rocks until eleven or so. This hour before school was Omar's favorite time of day. Before the visions started, he used to spend this time writing or thinking up stories. He wanted to be a published horror writer someday, and he knew he was good enough. But for now, his postings on Facebook were earning Omar plenty of fame, at least at Bridgewater High.

Omar poured himself a cup of black coffee and opened up his laptop. He wondered how many people had already commented on "Dead in Red."

"Eighteen comments," Omar read aloud. He tried not to smile. He hated to admit it, but compliments from his readers meant a lot to him.

Omar scrolled to the first comment. There was Jon with a smart-alec grin so big it just about broke his face in half. "You're sick, you know that?" it said.

"Thanks, Jon," Omar said out loud, and he meant it. Omar could count on his best friend for many things, and being the first to comment on Omar's stories was one of them.

Omar scrolled down further. The comments were pretty typical: "Awesome story, Omar!" "I totally felt like I was there!"

Omar had to admit, he didn't know exactly who a lot of these people were. Many were probably freshmen. Most were female. Omar always accepted friend requests from his readers. He checked to see his latest tally—he had 1,145 friends.

Omar kept scrolling to the bottom. Posted two minutes ago was a comment by Sophie Minax. He recognized her face. She was that Goth girl who was always watching him in the halls. Omar looked at her picture for a minute. She stared intently at the camera—though maybe it was just the effect of her thick black eyeliner. The right side of her face was covered by her purple-black hair. Her black lips curled into the slightest hint of a smile.

Sophie's comment was just a link. Omar clicked on it, and it took him to her profile.

Under "Sophie's pictures" was the heading, "For Omar." Below it was a pen-and-ink drawing done in thousands of tiny black lines. *Crosshatch,* Omar remembered the word from art class. You could change the pattern of lines to show depth, texture, and light.

Omar's hands fell off the keyboard as he looked at Sophie's drawing of the final scene from "Dead in Red." There was the beach, the dazzling water, the contrasting dark boots. The images were so vivid. There was the victim's hair—each strand really looked like it was floating away from her down-turned head.

"Amazing," Omar typed in his comment. For once, someone had really gotten one of his stories. Sophie had lived inside it. She'd understood it. It was like she'd seen what he'd seen in his vision.

By the end of the school day, Omar's coffee had worn off. He was a walking zombie. After school, he looked around for Jon, more out of habit than anything else. Maybe he'd skip hanging out this afternoon. Go on home. Get some sleep—if the visions would just stay away.

"Hey, Omar. Wait up." Jon fell into step beside Omar.

"Jon." Omar nodded at his friend, snapping out of his haze. "Sorry. Late night last night." They left the school grounds and turned toward the marina, their afternoon ritual.

"Little brother again?"

"Yeah. Plus the story . . ." Omar wanted to tell Jon about his visions. It felt strange to keep something hidden from his best friend.

"You can't help being a tortured artist, man."

Omar smiled. "I guess you're right."

After that, they walked in silence until they turned at the corner of Main Street and Marina.

"Loser pays," called Jon. He took off running. His feet slapped the pavement hard, but Omar passed him just before he reached the Chowder Hut.

"Loser," Omar taunted. "Your turn." He stepped inside the tiny restaurant ahead of Jon and sat by the window overlooking the water.

The marina was deserted this afternoon. The smell of fish drifted through the open window. Waves slapped the stony breakwater holding the pier. In minutes, a basket of fried clams and onion rings arrived at their table.

"Hey, Jon," Omar tried to make his voice sound casual. "Do you know that Goth girl, Sophie Minax? Probably a freshman?"

"Purplish hair?" Jon stretched and leaned back in his chair.

"Yeah."

"Total psycho."

"What? Come on, Jon. I'm serious."

"So am I. Did you know that she got sent home the other day for wearing some kind of dress made out of garbage bags?" Jon shook his head a little. Then he added, "Okay, not a psycho. A freak."

Omar laughed. "She's an amazing artist."

"I hear she's a Dumpster diver," Jon continued. "Half her clothes come from the parking lot outside Lucky Pizza."

"Jon," Omar began his retort. "You just can't handle a creative, independent woman who—"

The vision hit Omar with a physical shove. He slammed against the back of his chair and put his hands over his face.

"Omar—are you okay?" Jon looked scared.

Omar opened his eyes to see a boat exploding in flames.

"Jon," Omar managed to say. "I'm sorry. I've got to get out of here."

Omar heard his chair smack against the floor as he pushed away from the table. Then he just ran—out the door, past the water, down the street to his house. Bridgewater was a grey backdrop to the vision that made Omar's heart feel like it was breaking through his ribs.

The next thing Omar knew, he was typing at his laptop in his upstairs bedroom. As he wrote, the vision slowly drained from his body. His heart slowed. His hands stopped shaking. The light and the objects around him resolved back to normal color and shape.

Omar Phillips
"Ferry to Hell"
Friday, November 5, 2010, at 4:36 P.M.

That morning at the marina, the sky was especially hazy. The ferry commuters were too bleary-eyed to notice, though. At 7:00 A.M. everything feels hazy. But I noticed that the haze had a greenish tinge.

I watched the stream of faces walking up the metal plank into the passengers' area. Guys in suits. Families with kids in sweatpants. A few tourists left over from the summer season. A mom with a sleeping baby in a stroller.

We all settled into our vinyl seats, respecting each other's personal space. Out came the newspapers, the books, the snacks, the baby bottles. But I just wanted to look out the window and watch the waves crashing rhythmically against the edge of the boat.

I guess that's why I was the first to notice something strange off in the water. At first, all I noticed was that the waves looked different some distance from our boat. They were foamier, choppier—they were sloshing against the rhythm of the other waves. Then some of the waves started to rise. It was like the sky was pulling up the water. I looked up. A tall black cloud hovered above the area.

All at once, a funnel-shaped arm dropped down from the cloud. It swayed above the water for a minute or two. Then the arm touched down, and everything came fast. The water started to spin. It rose up into a swirling column, making a huge dent in the surface below it. It rode that dent, swaying on top of it, like someone balancing on a skateboard.

There was no time to warn the others. In a second, the thing was on top of us. Windows shattered, and the icy water rushed in. In an instant, it was up to my knees. Then, before the panic broke out—boom!—and the smell of gas. The next thing I knew, flames were sliding all over the surface of the water. One jumped up the sleeves of one of the businessmen. I smelled his burning hair. Shards of metal were flying through the *air too. I ducked down as one came hurtling toward my neck. It passed me, but it made a clean slice through a nearby woman's arm.*

That's when people started jumping overboard, and I saw things a person should never have to see. The woman with the baby zipped him up in her jacket and just dropped off the boat's edge. Others jumped in, crying and screaming. Some just went limp in the crowd and got shoved overboard. From where I was, they were just a bunch of flailing arms and bobbing heads. Then, one by one, the heads started disappearing.

The next day was Saturday. That was the day everything changed for Omar.

It started with his mom waking him up early.

"Omar," she whispered. "Omar, honey?" She was sitting on the edge of his bed, stroking his hair. Her eyes were red, though that was nothing new. But this morning she seemed even more slumped over than usual.

Omar shot up. "Mom! Where's Gabriel? What time is it?" Omar grabbed his glasses and squinted at the red numbers on the alarm clock. It was only seven o'clock. "What are you doing up, Mom?!"

"It's Natasha," his mom said.

Natasha. Omar tried not to think of that name too often. Natasha Monroe and her parents lived just a few houses down the block from Omar's family. Melissa Monroe, Natasha's mother, was probably the best friend Omar's mom had. Melissa was the one who'd brought over casseroles every day after his dad left and his mom couldn't get out of bed. She was the one he heard his mom whispering to on the phone in the middle of the night when she couldn't sleep.

Omar and Natasha had practically been brother and sister when they were little. Family photos all over Omar's house showed the two of them together—in a backyard pool, wearing matching sweatshirts at the zoo, side by side on playground swings. Then, a few years ago, things started to get weird between them. He'd heard Melissa and his mom laughing about it.

"It was bound to happen," Melissa had said.

"Teenage hormones," his mom agreed, laughing.

Then last year, he and Natasha had started dating after winter break. Maybe they knew too much about each other. Maybe the whole family connection was too weird. After a few weeks, Natasha had broken it off. She said Omar was "too intense." She "wasn't ready."

Omar cringed as he remembered what had happened next. He'd taken the breakup hard. Then one night, a few weeks after Dad had left, Omar tried drinking for the first time in his life. Somehow he'd ended up standing on Natasha's lawn, yelling things at her window that he couldn't remember later. Natasha's father, Bill Monroe, was an officer with the Bridgewater police. He'd taken Omar downtown and booked him, just to teach him a lesson.

"Stay away from my daughter," he'd said to Omar, shoving him into a holding cell and slamming the door shut. Omar sobered up fast in that cell while he waited for his mom to come pick him up. Ever since that night, Omar had heeded Officer Monroe's words—as much out of fear of Natasha's father as from his own shame.

His mom didn't say anything for a minute. She just sat there on the bed, looking at her hands. It was like she was so used to bad news—this most recent edition could easily wait just one more minute. When she looked up, her eyes were wet.

"Omar," she began again, "Natasha's missing. . . . She went on a date last night with a new boy, a boy she met on Facebook." Long pause. "Melissa begged her not to go. She ordered her not to go. But Natasha went anyway, and now she hasn't come home."

Omar waited for his brain to make sense of what was happening.

"Bill's organizing a search party," his mom continued. "The babysitter will be here any minute. I'm going to help, and you are too."

There were at least a dozen neighbors gathered outside the Monroe house. Officer Monroe thanked everyone for coming, for helping out during his family's "hour of need." You could tell he was all broken up in his own tough way. Then he got down to business. He collected cell-phone numbers and handed out maps showing everyone's search areas. He nodded at Omar as he handed him his map, and for the first time in months, Omar looked Bill Monroe in the eyes.

The search party spread out. Omar and his mom had the western shore of Lake Pinquot and the surrounding woods. Omar knew the area well—he and

Natasha had spent many happy hours hanging out in those woods when they were little.

Omar and his mom walked through the woods in silence. Though it had been a long time, it still felt familiar to him, keeping step with her along these paths. As the woods got thicker, the shade darkened into long, dense patches. His mom shivered, and Omar gave her his coat.

"Natasha!" Omar's mom called out. "Natasha, honey . . . it's Janine and Omar. Can you hear us?"

"Natasha!" Omar yelled as loud as he could. Officer Monroe had told them that search parties had more success when they called out for the person, but the whole thing made Omar jumpy. He hated calling and not getting any answer. His mom must have felt the same way too, because in a few minutes they were back to keeping their silent rhythm.

They walked for maybe an hour, jumping at every snapping branch, but mostly just listening to their own soft footprints. By now, the sun was high overhead. Omar's forehead glistened with prickly beads of sweat, and he stopped for a second to mop his face with his sleeve.

That's when Omar noticed a giant rock. He recognized it immediately—it was the rock from his

vision. Omar looked around. He hadn't realized it
before. These woods—he'd been here in his vision.
They were the backdrop for "Dead in Red."

Omar shivered.

"You want this back?" Omar's mom motioned to
the jacket around her shoulders.

"No, Mom," Omar said. He walked slowly to the
rock. For a second, he just stood there.

"What do you see, Omar?" His mom rushed over.

Omar couldn't force his eyes down.

"Omar!" his mom whispered. She pointed at the
far side of the boulder. On the ground was a clump
of human hair. "Natasha's hair." She choked on the
words. A few feet away were dark marks in the soil.
They led down a path toward the beach.

"She was dragged from here," his mom said.
She took off running along the trail of drag marks.
"Natasha! Natasha!" she shrieked.

But Omar didn't yell. He knew already that
Natasha couldn't hear him. During the next few
minutes, Omar felt like he was watching himself in a
movie. He saw his mother running toward the beach.
Against the sparkling water, her body made a frantic
silhouette. Then he lost sight of her through the
trees. A second later, he heard her scream. Omar ran

toward her. He felt his heart pounding. He heard his own quick breaths, branches snapping under his feet.

Then Omar was holding up his mother with both arms. They were at the shore, standing in the spot from his vision. Omar lifted his head and looked out on the lake.

There was Natasha. Facedown in the water. Her hair floated out in all directions. The sun glistened off her flame-red boots.

Omar closed his eyes. The story of his vision had come true.

Omar's mom called Bill, and in a few minutes the police were on the scene. Omar watched them coming—flashes of blue closing in on him from the woods behind him. *Run,* Omar's brain told him.

"I've got to get out of here," he said to his mom.

"Sure, Omar. You do what you need to do." One thing about his mom—she understood that everyone handled bad news their own way.

Then Omar was running, away from the lake, away from the police. The jumpiness in his muscles drained away in smooth, long strides. Omar's feet pounded on the dirt, then on the paved roads of town.

"Jon!" Omar stopped in front of his best friend's house. He started yelling before he reached the doorbell. "Jon! Open up, Jon!"

"Dude, I'm coming!" Omar heard Jon's footsteps on the stairs inside. Then the door swung open. "What the—? Omar, what happened?"

As Omar told Jon about Natasha, Jon slowly sank lower and lower until he was sitting on the concrete stoop outside. Jon looked small, sitting there, his oversized clothes drooping off his shoulders and knees. Jon put his head in his hands, and Omar sat down next to him. For several minutes, the two sat silently side by side.

"Jon . . . listen." Omar looked at his feet. "This is my fault. I got Natasha killed. Writing the story on Facebook. . . . It was like it came true."

Jon swung around to face Omar. "Man, don't be ridiculous." Jon's voice was almost angry. "It was just a creepy coincidence."

"No," Omar insisted. "If I hadn't written that story, she wouldn't have died."

Jon shot up. He looked his regular size again,

facing off against his best friend. "What? You think you have supernatural powers now? Is that it?" Jon was yelling, gesturing his arms in wide circles. "You think this is about you, Omar? About your *story?*" Jon stomped inside the doorway. "Not everything's about you, Omar." Jon grabbed the edge of the door. "Life is freaky. Deal with it," he said, just before he slammed it shut.

Omar blinked as the wind from the moving door brushed against his face. Then, he realized, a slight weight had lifted off his shoulders. Maybe Jon was right. This wasn't about him. *Life is freaky,* Omar repeated Jon's words in his head. The thought was strangely comforting.

"Jon!" Omar shouted again. "You're right! I'm sorry!"

Jon opened the door halfway. He looked at Omar with red eyes. "Sorry I freaked, man. It's just that—I'm just in a bad place right now."

"It's okay, Jon," Omar said. "I've got to get home, anyway." Natasha was dead, but Omar would let that news sink in later. Right now, Melissa needed his mom more than ever, and somebody would need to take care of Gabriel.

Omar forced himself to wake up early the next morning. He didn't care if he was tired. He needed some time alone before his mom and Gabriel woke up.

The sun was just rising as Omar made his way down into the kitchen. His laptop was sitting on the kitchen counter. Omar turned it on and slid onto a stool.

The story of Natasha's death was all over the news. The *Bridgewater Gazette* ran a special in-depth report. Omar skimmed the story on his monitor, looking for any new details. "Finding the killer is our number-one priority," Sheriff Sean Brady was quoted as saying. "By now the perpetrator has undoubtedly changed his identity and may even be planning his next attack. But our agents are combing the scene for evidence. We are confident that the Facebook stalker will be brought to justice."

Omar skimmed down. More quotes by officials: ". . . parents alarmed . . . raises questions about social-networking sites." Officer Monroe said, "Mark my words. I'm going to find this bastard before, God forbid, he preys on someone else's daughter."

Omar was just about to close his laptop when an accompanying story caught his eye. The headline read, "Teenage Neighbor Predicts Attack?" Omar clicked on the story and read:

"In what appears to be a bizarre coincidence, a Bridgewater teenager apparently wrote a fictionalized version of the stalker's attack one day before it happened. Omar Phillips is a neighbor and classmate of Natasha Monroe's. Well-known among his peers for his somewhat disturbing and off-color works of fiction, Phillips had posted 'Dead in Red' late Thursday night. In the story, a girl in 'flame-red' boots describes her 'date from hell' in which—"

Someone was pounding at the door. Omar got up to answer it. As he grabbed the handle, it swung open from the other side. Two hands grabbed Omar by the shoulders. They twisted his shirt into two knots. Then Omar was lifted off the ground. Two inches from Omar's face was a blurry Officer Monroe.

"You think this is funny?" Officer Monroe's spit rained down lightly on Omar's forehead. "This is your idea of some sick joke?" Monroe shook Omar and then dropped him back down. "You perverted little—" Monroe lifted his right arm, and Omar covered his face with both hands. He waited, heart pounding, for the blow, but nothing came. When Omar uncovered his face, Monroe was staring at him; his pinched dark eyes showed a mix of pure disgust and pure hatred.

"Mr. Monroe, I'm so sorry—" Omar began, but Monroe wasn't listening.

"I need answers . . . *now.*" Monroe walked into the kitchen and sat down heavily on one of the kitchen chairs. He leaned across the table, pushing Omar's laptop onto the floor with one of his elbows. Omar winced. "Where were you on the night of the incident?" Monroe said. He was in police mode now. He even pulled out one of the little notebooks that officers are always using on TV.

Omar thought a minute. He'd written "Ferry to Hell" after school. Then his mom had taken Gabriel to a friend's while she filled in a night shift at the restaurant. "I was at home," Omar said at last.

"Can anybody verify that?"

"No, sir," he said. Then, for a second, everything went black. Omar heard footsteps, breaking branches. He was back in the woods, but he smelled salt water this time. *Not now,* Omar begged his brain, *please, no vision now.*

"You didn't talk to anyone, text anyone?"

"I was pretty tired," Omar said. There was something in the darkness. Omar felt its heat on the back of his neck.

"Tired? From what?"

From going crazy, Omar wanted to say.

Monroe got up and grabbed Omar's foot. "These the shoes you were wearing?" He pulled off Omar's sneaker and held the sole up close to his eyes.

"Yes, sir." Didn't Monroe need a warrant or something to do stuff like that?

Monroe grunted and threw the shoe down.

"Let me see that." Monroe picked up Omar's laptop from the floor and opened it up.

"When was the last time you talked to Natasha? Do you communicate on Facebook?"

"No!" Omar yelled. Someone was getting hurt. In his vision, something was attacking in the dark. Omar saw red, glowing fingers around a neck.

Omar grabbed the laptop out of Monroe's hands. He jumped away and spoke quickly before the vision overtook him. "Look, Mr. Monroe, I'm sorry about Natasha, but . . . life is just freaky. I would never hurt Natasha. I loved Natasha. I don't know why I wrote that story. It just came to me . . ."

Monroe's head tilted as if he were considering an idea. He walked up to Omar so that the toes of his black shoes and Omar's one shoe and one sock were touching. Monroe looked hard at Omar for a second.

He can't book me, Omar thought. Monroe needed more evidence—and he knew it.

Finally, Monroe grunted and put his pad back in his shirt pocket. "I've got my eyes on you," he said. Omar felt Monroe's hot breath against his forehead. "You're not going to get away with this."

As soon as Monroe was out the door, Omar collapsed on the kitchen floor as the vision overtook him. When Omar came to, he found himself at his computer at the end of a story.

Omar Phillips
"Death Dive off Bluff Island"
Sunday, November 7, 2010, at 8:41 A.M.

"Where r u?" I punched the letters into my phone. The air had an edge tonight. It wasn't just the usual November-evening chill on Bluff Island, either. I didn't

like this feeling. I didn't like any feeling that I didn't understand. But this one made me especially uneasy. And besides, where the hell was Kellner? We were supposed to meet up at Dead Man's Cave, and Kellner was bringing the brewskies.

Dead Man's Cave. The name fit my mood perfectly. I slumped inside its opening and leaned my head against its cool stone side. I stretched out my legs. Just a short distance beyond my feet, the ground ended. The top of the bluff looked frosted tonight, like a horizon to another world.

I shivered. I remembered the story my brother Dan had told me. Dead Man's Cave was named after all those who'd come here to end their lives. "Jumpers," Dan had called them. Every ten years or so, the authorities would find another body. Always a young male, around fifteen. His body would be beaten up pretty bad from the fall, but there was always something else too—burn marks in a ring around his neck.

I realized I was rubbing my neck with one hand. I laughed a little. "Urban legend," I thought. I checked my watch. "C'mon, Kellner."

Snap! I heard footsteps in the underbrush behind

me. "Dude! Finally!" I said, standing up to meet my friend. But when I stepped out into the moonlight, I didn't see anyone coming up the path.

More breaking branches. More footsteps.

"Hello?" I called, turning in all directions.

"Heeeeelllllloooooooo." The reply was just a whisper. I could feel warm breath on the back of my neck.

I spun around. "Cut it out, Kellner!" I lunged at the space behind me, but my fist only punched the black air.

"Kellner, I'm going to kill—"

I couldn't breathe. It felt like a crushing weight was on top of me, but my feet were off the ground. I could see my body, hanging limp. Someone—something—was lifting me up by the neck. I could see my attacker's reddish arms, as thick as tree trunks.

The arms started to glow. At first it was so dim, I thought it was the shifting moon. But the glowing got brighter and brighter until it hurt too much to look at it. That's when the burning started.

The fingers around my neck seared my skin. I couldn't breathe long enough to scream. My body registered my horror by writhing and flailing. The giant arms lifted me to the edge of the bluff. For a second, I dangled there. I looked down and saw the water make *a backdrop to my legs and feet. Then the burning was gone from my neck, replaced by cool wind blowing against my skin and hair. I was falling. Below, the rocks got bigger and bigger until—SMACK! I heard the crunch of my own bones breaking.*

O mar managed to keep to himself the rest of the day. He pretended he was sleeping in his room. But avoiding his mom and Gabriel was easy anyway. Through his closed door, he could hear the downstairs sounds of cartoons and his mom talking on the phone. Omar knew she was comforting Melissa. He knew he should go downstairs, go help with Gabriel. But his mom didn't ask for help, and Omar had too much to take in right now: first the visions, then Natasha, then Monroe.

Omar didn't know how to feel this bad. He'd never felt this heartsick before, even after Dad left.

A physical ache radiated out from the middle of Omar's chest, pinning him to his bed.

The next morning, school was closed, thankfully. Students were encouraged to come in and talk with grief counselors, but Omar just wanted to be by himself. Around seven o'clock, he managed to drag himself out of bed and go downstairs. A few minutes later, though, his mom and Gabriel were walking around upstairs. Omar groaned.

"Omar—you up?" his mom was calling, but she knew the answer already. "Can you help me get Gabriel ready?"

Omar's mom had found an emergency opening at the day-care center downtown. After she dropped off Gabriel, she'd head to Melissa's to help with funeral arrangements.

"You okay all by yourself today?" she asked Omar.

Okay all by himself? Sometimes Omar wondered if his mother even knew him at all. "Yeah, sure, Mom," he said, turning back toward his open laptop as if to prove it.

Maybe he'd even be able to write today, he thought. Maybe he'd write something for Natasha, something beautiful. Omar closed his eyes as memories of Natasha flashed behind them, one after another. Maybe he'd write something good enough to read at her funeral.

Omar wrote all morning. He'd managed only to do it, to write what he felt without thinking too much about it. When he was done, he read over his work. It was good.

The sick ache in Omar's chest was gone, at least for now. For the first time since Saturday morning, Omar felt like eating. He flipped on the TV in the kitchen. He spooned cereal into his mouth, half-listening to a story about fall colors.

"This just in—" There was a shift in the newscaster's voice. Omar turned his attention to the screen.

"It appears that a bizarre and deeply disturbing accident has befallen travelers to Bluff Island this morning," the newscaster was saying. "Standing by is Michelle Stamford with more details regarding the tragic fate of the 7:00 A.M. ferry commuters. Michelle—we're hearing that the ferry encountered some sort of rare and devastating natural disaster?"

"That's right, Jim. Authorities are calling it a water funnel, which is essentially a tornado that touches down over the ocean. It's incredibly rare in this climate."

"I see medical personnel carrying stretchers behind you. What kind of casualties are we talking about here?"

"Well, Jim, reports are still coming in, but it's sure to be in the dozens, at least. Apparently, the event set off a gas explosion, and passengers in the main area were trapped in the fire. Others were injured by objects carried inside the water funnel—like flying missiles, if you will. I have one survivor here who says many jumped overboard out of desperation—including one mother with her newborn baby zipped up inside her coat. Young man," the reporter turned to address the person standing next to her, "you've seen some terrible things today. What can you tell us?"

The camera turned to frame the person the reporter had addressed, but Omar already knew who was standing there, what he would say, what he had felt. On the screen in Omar's kitchen was the narrator from his story.

Omar dropped his bowl, shattering the glass and spreading cereal across the floor. "Ferry to Hell" had come to life.

That afternoon the hate mail started. On Facebook, Omar had twenty new messages and thirty new comments on "Ferry to Hell" alone.

Omar scrolled down through his messages. He didn't recognize many of the senders' names or their pictures.

"You are one twisted freak," the first message read.

"This is seriously messed up."

"God will punish you."

Omar kept scrolling down. More disbelief, more disgust. One person had written simply, "What are you?"

Omar closed his eyes. "I don't know," he whispered.

Uh, Omar?"

Omar flinched. He turned to see Jon standing in the kitchen doorway.

"I guess you didn't hear me knock," Jon said.

Omar didn't say anything. He didn't like the fake-casual sound in Jon's voice.

"Uh, Omar?" Omar's silence made Jon awkward. He sat across from Omar at the kitchen table. "I gotta ask you something."

Omar met Jon's gaze. For a second, he saw Jon as he'd looked the first time they'd met in middle school. Jon had looked like a fifth-grader at best, with blonde spikes sticking out all over his head. But he made up for it with a big, easy personality. That day, Jon's face was nothing but a big smile and clear blue eyes.

"Omar, this is tough."

Omar returned to the present Jon, the one who looked red-eyed and tired.

"I was at school today . . . for help about Natasha, you know?" Jon continued. "There were a lot of kids there." Jon paused between each sentence. "People at school—the kids I was with—they think that you had something to do with her . . . and the ferry too.

"I mean, I know they were just stories—" Jon looked at Omar questioningly. "I know I got mad at you before when you said you had something to do with Natasha, but now—"

Jon was looking for something. He was waiting for Omar to reassure him, but Omar couldn't say whatever it was Jon was looking for.

"A lot of people got hurt, Omar." Jon's words sounded like an accusation.

"I've got to go, Jon," Omar said at last. He had to get away from here. Away from the TV, from Facebook, away from the scared look in Jon's eyes.

"Sure, okay," Jon said in that casual voice again.

He shoved his hands in his pockets and headed out without looking back.

Omar waited for Jon to walk out of sight before standing up. Then he grabbed his coat and phone and headed out. He stopped and turned back for his laptop. Omar didn't know where he was going or what he was going to do. Maybe he'd be able to write. Maybe he was too messed up even for that.

He headed blindly toward the front door and clawed at the door's bolted lock. Finally, the lock clicked and the door swung open, but Omar couldn't move. A blue cruiser was parked by the curb in front of his house. There was Monroe, in uniform, coming out of the driver's side. Another officer was already coming up the walkway.

Omar slammed the door shut. He bolted the lock again. Then he ran out the back door, through his yard, to the fence.

"Omar Phillips!" Monroe was running around the side of the house. "I have a warrant to search the premises, Omar!"

Omar reached up and curled his fingers over the top of the wooden fence. He easily pulled himself up and swung lightly over the top.

"Go ahead and run, Omar!" Monroe called. He was standing in Omar's backyard. "I'm a patient man, Omar." His voice sounded like he was smiling. "A patient man with a mission. I'll be right here waiting for you when you come back."

Omar headed toward the woods. Instinctively, he walked in the direction of a clearing several miles in. Sunlight streamed through the branches overhead and fell in mottled stripes across his chest. In the distance, he could hear the faint crashing sound of a brook running over rocks. Omar tried to take in the peace of this place, but nothing could reach him through the static in his brain. It only hurt more to be here, to see this, and to have it feel so out of reach.

Omar was at the edge of the clearing when he lost control of his hands. For a second, they froze, bent at the fingers like claws. Then they started twisting. Omar felt flesh squeezing between his fingers. Then a gurgling sound. In his vision, he was squeezing someone's neck. As his thumbs crushed the windpipe, he heard his victim cry out.

Omar was kneeling now. His knee was pressing on someone's chest. Omar looked down. It was Monroe. Monroe's face was turning purple. Red lines crisscrossed the whites of his eyes, as blood vessels popped beneath the surface. Monroe was crying too. His tongue lolled from his mouth as he tried to beg for his life. Omar felt Monroe's drool. He felt Monroe's tears and spit coating his fingers.

"No!" Omar screamed. He yanked his arms away from Monroe's neck. He grabbed the sides of his head and started spinning, as if he could shake the vision away.

"Write it." Just above the edge of consciousness, Omar detected a voice in his head. He knew that voice. Not male or female. Not young or old, but slightly electronic. It buzzed in the circuits of his brain. He had heard it before. When? As Omar hesitated, the voice grew more insistent.

"Write it," it said again.

Omar peered into the blackness of his memory.

"Write it!" The voice was almost screaming now. As the answer jumped into Omar's mind, he gasped. "Dead in Red." He'd heard the voice while writing "Dead in Red." And then again—Omar jumped up. He'd heard it again while writing "Ferry to Hell" and then again while writing "Death Dive off Bluff Island."

Omar stopped, remembering "Death Dive." The narrator had been waiting for "Kellner." Why was that name so familiar? Who was it? Omar closed his eyes to think.

Kellner . . . Kellner . . . Suddenly, the laughing face of Jon's older cousin came to Omar. Then he saw the dangling figure from the bluff, the red fingers around the figure's throat. Omar scanned the moonlit face that appeared in his mind.

Omar shot up. He knew that face. Jon! "Death Dive" was about Jon!

O mar spun around looking for his laptop. It was lying in a clump of leaves several feet away. Omar raced over, unzipped the case, and turned it on. There was the file—"Death Dive off Bluff Island."

What a crappy title, Omar thought. He barely remembered writing it. As he scrolled down, he skimmed the story. Most of it felt just as unfamiliar. But this was no time for rewriting. Omar had to change the ending—no searing fingers, no rocks, no snapping bones.

Omar started to edit the final scenes. His fingers tapped expertly on the keyboard. This is what

Omar loved about writing stories. You could change anything. Its whole universe was up to him. Instead of a cliff, a street. Instead of rocks, trees. Instead of death, life.

Omar stopped to review his work. He peered at the monitor. Not a word had changed. Maybe something was wrong with his computer. Omar carefully typed *Breaker Street* over *Bluff Island* in the file. For a second, his edit glowed at him from the monitor. But then it went back to *Bluff Island.* Omar tried again with other words, but the same thing happened. Cliff went back to cliff, rock to rock, and death to death.

Last year, in European History, Omar had been gripped by the story of lepers, those diseased people from the Middle Ages. Their fatal illness made their fingers and toes curl inward. They walked around with black bumps and red patches on their skin. Some went blind. Everybody thought lepers were contagious, so they were afraid of being around them. The lepers were separated from everyone else. They were moved into leper colonies to die together.

Omar wished there was a colony for people like him—cursed people without real families, who scared and disgusted those around them, who were hunted by the police. Omar had lost Natasha and now this. Writing—the one thing that eased the visions, the one thing he truly loved—killed the people around him.

But Omar didn't have time to feel sorry for himself. Another vision was coming over him. He was in this one, driving in his car. The night was so black. His foot pressed on the gas. He went faster and faster, around the corner, until the car stopped with a lurch. Omar had run over something. He got out to look. So foggy. He heard crying, that crying. There was his brother, under the tire, in a pool of blood.

"Write it, write it, write it."

"No!" Omar screamed.

"Please, Omar, write it." His brother's voice now, crying.

"Write it, Omar." His mother was there suddenly, holding his crying brother.

"You're not my brother! You're not my mother!" Omar screamed.

"Please, Omar," his brother said again.

"No, no. It's a trick. Stop it!" But Omar's hands had already picked up his laptop and opened it across his folded legs. A file was opened, and Omar's fingers were flying over the keys. Omar lifted his hands away, but instantly they were brought back down again. He squeezed his fingers into fists, but they uncurled and starting tapping lightly again. Omar watched the words appearing, spilling into neat black lines across the monitor.

"No!" From some primal pit inside him, a roar erupted. Hands still typing, Omar pushed the laptop off his legs and onto the ground. He kneeled in front of it to brace himself. Omar's whole body coursed forward, then with a shove back, his hands released themselves from the keys.

Omar picked up the computer and lifted it over his head, throwing it as hard as he could. The computer smacked against a tree and fell to the ground, bouncing a couple of times. Still, the screen was lit. Omar bounded over to the tree. Then, with another yelp, he raised one bent leg and brought the heel of his boot crashing down on the monitor. The screen went black, but Omar kept twisting his heel. He savored the crunching sound, the gravelly feel of broken glass under his feet. Omar didn't care if he ever wrote again.

"What's happening to me?" Omar whispered. His mind started spinning. What was he going to do? How could he stop the visions? How could he keep the people he loved safe?

"There's no way out," Omar whispered at last. He curled to the side and hugged himself around the middle with both arms. "I need to die."

You can't die."

Someone was approaching Omar from behind. Omar didn't recognize her high, musical voice. As her shadow fell across Omar's face, he shot up.

"What did you say?" He spun around.

There was Goth girl Sophie Minax, the one with the Facebook drawing of "Dead in Red." She was dressed all in black—shiny, plastic boots, long black skirt with black sequins, black ribbed tank top. Her black lips opened into a bright smile.

"I said, 'You can't die.' "

Omar didn't know where to begin. "What the hell—" he started to say, but a shot exploded in his ears. Omar jumped back. A smoking pistol flashed in Omar's mind. He shook his head violently, trying to clear the image.

Sophie peered at him through the purple hair. "Is it a bad one?"

Omar blinked and looked down at her. "You know the visions?"

"Of course." She sat down on the ground. She stretched her legs in front of her and leaned back on propped elbows. "I'm one of you."

Omar writhed and screamed as the vision took over. Sophie knelt down next to Omar. She stroked his hair, murmuring softly, "They're hard to live with, aren't they?"

Omar looked into Sophie's dark eyes, gentle and concerned. Their deep gold flecks glinted in the light, and the blinding spin of images disappeared. The smell of smoke was gone. Omar's head felt light as the vision ended abruptly.

"What do you mean, 'one of you'? What are we? What's happening to me? Why can't I die?" Omar blurted out.

"Slow down, Omar. We have lots of time." She studied his face with an interested smile. Sophie pulled Omar by the hand. "Let's walk." They headed

down a path deeper into the woods. Omar leaned
into Sophie. She smelled like damp earth and burning
wood, but there was another scent too, like chemicals
or maybe paint.

Omar gripped Sophie's hand as they walked
deeper into the forest. There was no path, but Sophie
obviously had a destination, turning at specific points
along the way. As they walked, the sun lowered in the
sky.

"You and I are members of a special . . . how shall
I put it?" Sophie paused as she searched for the right
word. "A special . . . race, Omar," Sophie finished,
nodding a little. "We have special gifts—we're brilliant
artists. Like you, for example, with your writing and
me with my drawing. But our gifts . . . they have
betrayed us."

Betrayal, Omar thought. Yes, that was exactly how
it felt. "So I'm right then, Sophie?" he said. "My stories
are the cause—my stories killed Natasha and the ferry
commuters—"

"Yes, Omar, you are more powerful than you
know. How can I explain it?" Sophie stopped again as
if to pluck the right words from the air. "Our lives are
a tangled web of—yes, curses, Omar—but also gifts,"

Sophie continued. "We're practically immortal, you and I. Take me, for example. I'm hundreds of years old. I've experienced dozens of deadly accidents, fatal illnesses. None of it touched me—not even age can take its toll on us, Omar. There is no running away from our lot. We must learn to live with our powers, to fulfill the dream of who we are."

The dream of who we are? Sophie sounded crazy. And yet everything she said seemed to make sense of the horrors that surrounded him. Omar had so many questions; his mind riffled back to the first one. "But why *practically* immortal?" he said. "So we don't have to live forever?"

"There *is* one way we can die," Sophie said. "Many like us have died that way. In fact, you and I are the only two left, Omar. That's why we must rely on each other."

"Wait a minute. Slow down. How did they die? Why?"

"They couldn't stand the visions," Sophie replied. "They were weak. Not strong like you."

"I don't understand." Omar stopped walking. "I'm not strong."

Sophie looked sharply at Omar. "You are! I've

been watching you. I know you have a strong will—as strong as mine."

Omar scoffed. "Strong? All I want to do is die!" He stared out across the woods and his heart pounded. "Please, tell me how to do it."

"I can help you," Sophie said. "But I won't tell you how to die, Omar." She grabbed both of Omar's hands. She looked at Omar the way old people sometimes do—in that kind but remote way. Like she thought she remembered what he was going through but didn't really. "There is another way to stop the visions, Omar," she said. "It will not be easy. It will be the hardest thing you have ever done. I will tell you about it, but not until you are ready."

Omar had so many more questions for Sophie.

"What does that mean—ready? How will I be ready? Can you help me keep Jon safe—he's my best friend. He's the one in 'Death Dive—'" Omar began.

"Shhhhhh," Sophie interrupted. Omar noticed that she was crouched down a little. "You're scaring Hilda," she whispered.

There was a scampering in the leaves. Then, a flash of brown. Sophie swooped down. When she stood up, there was a brown, furry creature on her shoulder. Its long tail snaked down her back; its whiskers quivered against her neck.

"Ooooh, how's my baby?" Sophie cooed to the creature as she ran one finger down its sleek back. The animal nuzzled its pink nose in her neck, and Sophie threw back her head and laughed.

"Omar," she said, still laughing. "This is Hilda, my ferret."

When Hilda caught sight of Omar, she jumped off Sophie's shoulder and dived back into the underbrush. Omar and Sophie followed the animal into a large clearing. Omar thought that he knew these woods fairly well, but this place was unfamiliar. Huge old trees with trunks as wide as doors circled the area. The tops of the trees touched, creating a canopy of black branches overhead. Some of the trees were weeping willows, and they looked like low, bent heads over the ground. In the middle of the clearing stood a huge granite boulder. It spiked up into the sky like a monument.

"Sophie, it's so beautiful here—" Omar began. Then he stopped at the sight of a small structure on the far side of the clearing. Its sides looked almost orange in the slanting sun, but as Omar walked closer he saw that they were made of smooth sheets of metal. The roof was metal too, with sheets of glass that Omar realized were solar panels. A small metal tube with smoke curling out of it rose from the roof.

"You live here, Sophie?"

"Yes," Sophie said, pulling open the metal door. She ran her hand against the wall to find a switch, and the whole thing lit up from the inside. Omar stepped inside and gasped at what he saw. Every inch of every wall was covered in tiny lines—the same crosshatch from her picture on Facebook. Each line looked like it had been scratched into the metal— *etched,* Omar remembered the word—with a knife. Some lines were light and feathery; some were dark gashes. Obviously, the walls were covered with some kind of mural, but the detail was so intense that Omar couldn't make sense of it. For a second, Omar's eyes took in pieces of the whole—softness, curves or rough patches, watery surfaces, reflecting light, shadow. Omar pressed his back against one wall and focused on the opposite wall.

Faces. That's what it was. Hundreds of faces— angry, pensive, joyous, desperate faces. Omar slowly turned around. Faces covered the other walls as well. As Omar's eyes scanned the images, he noticed that as varied as the faces were, they were all similar in one way. Every one showed a teenager.

"Sophie! These are amazing!"

"Thanks," Sophie said lightly. "It's my most recent project—a collage of faces."

"All young faces," Omar added.

"Yes," Sophie said. "How perceptive of you. All my subjects are sixteen—the age at which I stopped growing older. I consider the piece a testament to my perpetual youth."

Sophie waved her arms toward a pile of colorful pillows against the far corner. "Have a seat, please."

Omar sat down awkwardly on the pile, and Sophie laughed a little. "I hate furniture. It's so . . . oppressive," she said with another wave of her hand.

Omar looked around. Besides the pillows, the only other "furniture" was a woodstove and a laundry basket spilling over with Sophie's clothes. Wires from a laptop on the floor led outside to some kind of solar-powered generator.

"Would you like some tea?" Sophie asked politely, and Omar noticed some mugs and other kitchen items in an orange milk crate beside the woodstove.

"Um, sure," Omar said. He watched Sophie pull out a clay jar and scoop some black leaves into the mugs. She took the kettle and went outside. When she came back, it was filled with water.

"Is there a well out there?" Omar asked.

"Yes," Sophie said, "the same well from when I was a kid." She looked around. "This is the site of my childhood home, Omar. . . . Of course, I've made a few updates."

"Where did you get all this stuff?" Omar asked.

"Some of it from Dumpsters." Sophie was pulling out a tray of some kind of biscuits from the stove. "It's amazing the waste, what people throw away in this society." Sophie put the tray down on top of the stove. "Some of it I—how shall I put this?—I took for my own benefit from undeserving others.

"I make do, Omar," Sophie continued. "You see I don't need much." Sophie pointed her chin toward the room. "I sew all my own clothes, and these pillows too. Sometimes I sell my drawings at craft fairs or do commissions for rich people."

Sophie handed Omar his tea and one of the biscuits on a plate. "This seems like hardship to you, Omar, but it isn't. I've suffered much worse; we all did."

"Who's we?" Omar asked, balancing his cup and plate on his lap.

"Me, my brother, my parents," Sophie said, "They all three died young, all in 1801. A smallpox epidemic. Everybody was dying from it back then, but not *me,* of course.

"It all seems so long ago now, Omar," she continued. "I've been on my own a long time. . . . I've been so lonely. Then I met you." Sophie sat down on the pillows next to Omar. She put her head against his shoulder. "You know you're a genius, don't you?" she said, looking up at him.

Suddenly Omar felt as if he didn't know what do with his own body. He kept his hands by his sides and sat stiffly upright. "How did you find me?" he said, eager to fill the awkward pause.

"It wasn't easy, Omar," Sophie said. "I've been looking for someone like me for a long time. That's why I was at Bridgewater High. I noticed you from your stories on Facebook. Then, when your stories started coming true, I saw you were like me."

"So your visions come true too?"

"They used to, when I drew them. I drew pictures of my visions, and they came true. That's how it works—through whatever your art is."

"But you said *used to,* Sophie. That means they stopped?"

"They stopped," Sophie said, "as they will for you, when you are ready."

S ophie wouldn't explain "ready." She had a way of dodging Omar's questions, laughing them off or distracting him with another topic. Talking to Sophie was like how Omar imagined it would be to swim in the open sea. Her words carried him off to faraway and deep waters. He struggled to keep up, but at the same time, she carried him along, and the views were amazing.

Little by little, Omar relaxed. As darkness fell, he slumped against the pillows, legs stretched out in front of him. Sophie's purple hair spilled across his chest. Through the skylight in her tiny, homemade shack, they watched the stars come out, one by one. They talked and talked until they felt they didn't have to. They lay together in the silence and the starry darkness.

It was seven o'clock when Omar's phone buzzed, and he jolted upright. "Gabriel!" he shouted. "Sophie! I'm sorry, I have to go home and watch my brother."

Sophie folded herself back up on the pillows. "It's okay, Omar." She was just a shape in the darkness.

"See you tomorrow?" Omar asked.

Suddenly Omar was blinking in bright light. Sophie was standing across from him. She leaned against a wall with her arms crossed. In her left hand she held a small knife with a round, wooden handle.

"I won't be coming to school anymore," she said, "now that you can come see me. . . . You remember the way here?"

Omar nodded. She looked at him intently, as if she were studying his face. Then she turned abruptly. With her feet, she pushed away the pillows to reveal a smooth, untouched patch of wall behind it. She knelt down in the corner and started etching.

"Okay, bye then," Omar said. "I'll come back

tomorrow after school." But Sophie didn't turn her head as Omar pulled open the small metal door and walked out into the dark woods.

Omar raced home. His legs carried him easily back over the dirt paths, the lit streets of town, and to his own front porch. He ran through the front door.

"Mom, I'm here!" he began, but he stopped suddenly at what he saw. His mom was sitting in the kitchen in her bathrobe. Gabriel was perched on her lap, red-eyed but at least not crying. They sat perfectly still, as if in contrast to the chaos around them.

"It was Bill," his mom said slowly and evenly. Omar knew this voice. It was the same slow, even tone she'd taken when his dad had left. "He came with a warrant," she continued. She pointed with her chin to the open cupboard doors, the upturned drawers, the papers spilling everywhere across the floor.

For the first time in months, Omar stopped and really looked at his mother. When had she gotten so thin? She'd stopped dyeing her hair too, he noticed, and white, coarse fringes shot out in spirals around her face. Suddenly, she looked so frail to him, sitting there amidst the mess of their lives. Omar felt like something was squeezing his chest.

"Mom!" he yelped.

"Listen, Omar," his mom began. It was barely a whisper. The quieter her voice got, the tighter the squeezing in Omar's chest got. "They didn't find anything." She gently lifted Gabriel and handed him to Omar. She wrapped her arms around both of them. "It will be okay. Everything *will* be okay."

Omar hugged her hard. "I don't know why those stories came true, Mom," he whispered. "It's like I'm cursed or something—"

"Don't say that, Omar!" his mom interrupted. "There's no evidence. You didn't do anything wrong!"

Omar smiled down at her. "You know, you're right, Mom," he said slowly. It was true. Whatever had happened—was happening—to Omar, it was all some kind of accident. But at least, because of Sophie, for the first time Omar agreed with his mom. Everything would be okay. The visions would stop. Jon *would* be okay.

Omar's mom made it to work, just in time, and
Gabriel fell asleep eventually. It was after 11:00, but
Omar wasn't tired. He worked late into the night,
slowly putting things away. For the first time in
weeks, the visions stayed away.

The next morning, Omar walked to school. As he approached, talk stopped. Kids parted to make a path for him as if he were toxic. Eyes down, Omar just focused on putting one foot in front of the next. He just had to make it through the day until he could get back to Sophie's.

After school, he raced through the woods. The days were getting shorter now, and cold—Omar could see the white puffs of his breath in the slanting sunlight. It was almost dark by the time he arrived. Sophie was waiting outside, wearing a dress that looked like scarves wrapped around her body. In the dusk, her shape looked like a sheath of shredded paper.

"Sophie!" Omar ran toward her black shape. She took a step back and gave him a tight little smile.

"You're late." Sophie's voice was vicious.

Omar just looked at her for a second. "Late . . . what do you mean?"

"I've been waiting for you!" Sophie shrieked.

"I'm sorry, Sophie, I just don't know what—"

"I worked all night for you—etching your portrait. I've welcomed you into my house—into my life! I've trusted you with my secrets, shared my gifts—and you disappoint me!" She took a long, shuddering breath. When she spoke again, Omar noticed that the edges of her lips were white. "The visions have been better today haven't they?"

"Yes—it's like I'm finally—"

"It's temporary." Sophie's voice was a slamming door. "It's just because you're happy now. But you'll get tired of me. Then the visions will come back, and they'll be worse. You'll disappoint me then."

"Sophie, what are you talking about?" He couldn't believe this was the same Sophie who had seemed so together yesterday.

"Omar!" Sophie reached up and grabbed Omar's face with both hands. "Are you ready to save Jon, to end all visions forever? Are you ready to do what I say?"

"Yes," Omar said quietly. He wasn't sure what he was getting himself into. But even with the leper treatment at school that day, he'd felt better than he had in a long time. "I'm ready."

"Omar, promise me. You must obey me. You must do as I say."

"I will. I mean, I'm trying to."

"Come with me." Suddenly normal again, Sophie led the way into her little house. The pillows had been moved, and a small lamp shone like a spotlight on the wall. It lit the area where Sophie had been working.

Omar walked up to the wall and crouched down to stare into his own face. The likeness was remarkable. There were his features exactly, his straight nose, the dent above his mouth, his dark eyebrows. Omar stared at the image for several seconds, tilting his head slightly to one side. . . . Something was off. His portrait was smiling, but he didn't look happy. His eyes had a knowing look. Omar knew that look—a look of satisfaction and despair all at once.

"Well, Omar?" He felt Sophie's presence behind him.

Omar turned around, and recognition hit him instantly. The familiar expression—it was Sophie's.

"You and I are one and the same, Omar," Sophie said. "That's why I drew you like that. To show you how you will be once you reach your true potential, the way I have."

Omar looked away; his stomach felt off suddenly, churning from impatience and a new feeling—dread. "What do I have to do, Sophie?" His voice was tired. "What is this awful thing you won't tell me?"

"You're going to be scared, Omar." Sophie pulled him down next to her on the cold floor.

"It's okay," Omar reassured her. "I'll do it. I'll do whatever I have to."

Sophie turned toward Omar. Half her face was lit up from the light that shone on Omar's portrait, but the opposite side was barely discernable under a dark shadow. She moved her face just inches from Omar's. "There's just one way to end the visions," she said, barely breathing her words. "By sacrifice. You must perform one sacrifice."

"What does that mean?" Omar said, leaning away slightly.

"You have to make one of the visions come true."

"But some *have* come true—the ones I wrote."

Sophie sighed. "Not like that Omar. You have to carry one out yourself."

I'd have to kill people?" Omar whispered.

"Only one," Sophie said. "Before the visions get worse."

Omar sat quietly for a minute. "Is that what you did?" he finally asked, though he knew the answer already. Of course. So that's what Sophie had meant by "ready"—ready enough to handle this little detail about her past.

Sophie nodded.

"Are you going to tell me about it?"

"No," Sophie said. Omar couldn't read her voice— no longer vicious but not normal either. He saw a blankness in her eyes he didn't recognize. And her face—Omar hadn't noticed before how her skin sagged around her ears and the corners of her eyes.

"That's okay. I don't think I really want to know anyway," Omar said, turning away from her. "Listen, Sophie, I think you got me wrong. I'm not ready. I don't think I'll ever be ready."

Sophie grabbed his arm and yanked him toward her. "You think you're better than me?" She practically spat out each word. That anger again. "You don't know how it was—you—you simpering, sniveling coward!"

"What's with you, Sophie?"

"You think you know me?" Sophie was shouting now. "You don't know anything."

Without a word, Omar stood up and turned to leave. Shoulders back and head high, he pulled open the metal door and entered the moonlit forest. He wasn't going to fight with her. He concentrated on the woods ahead of him and let Sophie's taunts hit the back of his stiff body.

"Disappoint me!"

"You make me sick!"

"Weak—weak like the others!"

The others. Omar had forgotten about them.

Sophie had said they couldn't take the visions. What did that mean, anyway?

Omar had barely made it out of the clearing when he felt something rubber knock gently against his face. He looked up into the sole of a shoe. It belonged to a corpse hanging from a noose above. No, it wasn't a corpse. It was still living—a woman gasping for air and clawing at her neck. "You, you, you!" the woman raised a limp arm and pointed it at Omar. "You did this."

"Sophie!" Omar screamed. He turned to run back, but now the clearing was ringed by dangling figures, squirming and jerking on their nooses.

"Sophie, make it stop!" Omar wrapped his arms around his body and closed his eyes, but the vision continued. He felt hands pulling at his clothes and hair.

"Write it." That familiar voice again, urging him on. Omar let the vision hit him, focusing now on staying in place. But his arms reached out and picked up a long, pointed stick. His feet started scraping the ground. Omar watched as they cleared a smooth patch of ground around him. Then Omar's arms lunged forward. With the stick, they began tracing letters into the smooth ground.

"No!" Omar threw the stick as far away as he could. He raced back into the clearing and pulled a low, thin branch off the side of a birch tree. Omar sat on the ground. With his left hand, he started winding the branch around his right arm and thigh, tying them together.

Omar's right side was tied into a ball, but his left arm and leg were clawing at the ground. Pain ran up and down Omar's left side as he was dragged toward the stick. "Please," Omar begged his body. "Please stop." But his left hand had grasped the stick, and the stick was digging deep grooves in the earth.

"Come on, Omar." Sophie's voice now, gentle. Sophie's hands on his shoulders. She must have led him to her cabin, because when Omar came to, he was lying on Sophie's pillows. His right arm hurt. Omar lifted up his sleeve and saw a row of purple bruises.

"What happened, Sophie?" he asked.

"You burst out of the strips you tied," Sophie

answered. "Then your left arm started pounding on your right arm."

"I didn't want to write it," Omar said.

"I know," Sophie said. "You didn't want to hurt all those people."

"I didn't write it, did I?"

"No, Omar, I wouldn't let you."

"Sophie!" Omar reached for her small frame. "My God, thank you."

"Omar—" Sophie began, stroking his hair. "Are you beginning to understand now? Don't you see how one sacrifice saves many?"

"Yes," Omar said. He did sort of understand, but still, he couldn't imagine killing someone innocent. "I'll have to think about it, Sophie."

Sophie thought she hid it, but Omar noticed: irritation showed for a second on her pinched lips before she forced them open into a smile.

"Of course," she said, "of course." Then she added, "You know you get to choose, don't you? Choose which sacrifice to make?"

"Okay," Omar said.

"I'm just saying, Omar." That irritation again. "It's not like you'd have to kill someone you liked. Didn't you have a vision about that creep Monroe? What about him? I'm just saying, Omar, maybe you'd be doing the world a favor."

Would Melissa appreciate the favor? His friends? Omar kept his mouth shut. He didn't want Sophie to feel him backing away, so he leaned in closer.

"I know what you're saying, Sophie," he lied, hoping he was better at hiding his true emotions than she was. Because the person inside him wanted to run from her and get the hell out of there forever. And it wasn't just that her remark sounded like something from some serial killer on the five o'clock news.

He hadn't told Sophie about his vision about Monroe. He hadn't told anyone.

Omar didn't know exactly what dark game Sophie was playing, but he knew he had to play along—at least until he could figure out the rules. Omar stayed at Sophie's cabin until seven, when she'd believe that he had to go home to watch his little brother. He even managed to say a normal good-bye and walk slowly away from her cabin until he was sure that she was no longer watching him.

Once it was safe, Omar leaned against a tree and grabbed for his phone. Omar punched in Jon's number. "Come on, Jon, pick up, pick up—"

"Omar?" Jon's voice was surprised.

"Jon!" Omar practically shouted.

Jon laughed a little. "Yeah, it's me, Omar. How's it going, man? I heard at school today that you hooked up with Goth girl—is that true?"

"Jon, listen to me," Omar interrupted. "I have to see you right away. Can you meet me at the Chowder Hut in a half an hour?"

"What's going on, Omar?"

"Jon," Omar said. "It's bad between me and Sophie."

"What are you doing hanging out with her anyway? You gotta end that. I mean . . . everyone already thinks you—"

Jon's voice broke off. But Omar knew what his friend almost said. "I know, Jon. I will. I mean, it's not that easy. . . . Listen, whatever you do, don't go to Bluff Island, okay?"

"What the hell are you talking about?" Jon said.

"I know. It sounds crazy. I'll explain everything."

"Dude!" Jon said. "I'm at the island now! Kellner's meeting me at Dead Man's Cave with the brewskies."

"Jon, listen to me." Omar spoke slowly. "You have to get out of there. *Now.*"

"Omar, you're freaking me out."

"Good. Just meet me at the Chowder Hut, okay?"

"Alright, alright," Jon said, "Just give me forty-five. . . . Oh, and Omar?"

"Yeah?"

"I'm sorry about your stories and the way I reacted."

"It's cool, Jon. Just *show up.*"

The woods were especially dark tonight. Omar couldn't even see his own legs, but he could hear his feet cracking branches and shuffling leaves. He heard the night sounds of the other nocturnal animals too. The crisp fall air made his cheeks sting and his eyes water. Omar remembered how he'd always loved the night, and even now, he was amazed that it could be a comfort to him.

Omar knew he had a lot of things to figure out—about the others, about how Sophie knew about the Monroe vision, about what she wanted him to do. About her vicious streak.

But Omar had enough experience with big problems to know that you couldn't tackle them all at once. No, you had to break them down or they'd make you useless. Right now Omar had to save Jon. He'd deal with Sophie later.

Damn! Omar thought as he caught a glimpse of fire in the edges of his sight. *Not now.* Omar braced himself for the oncoming vision. He quickly took off his jacket and removed his T-shirt. Using his teeth, he tore it into strips. While he could, he used the strips to tie one hand to a raised tree root. With the other arm, he grabbed onto the tree as hard as he could.

He was getting good at this by now—he wasn't even afraid of what he'd see. As long as he could get through the images without writing them down, he could handle it.

Here we go, Omar thought as he felt the heat prickle his skin, as the smell of burnt rubber made him cough and gag.

"Write it!" the voice told him, and Omar yelled back, "No!"

"Write it!"

"No, no, no."

Omar's brain was resisting, but he'd lost control of his body. He was standing now, using the full force of his legs and both his hands to pull up the tree root. The tree root bent up into a steep arc, then it snapped. Omar took off like an unleashed dog, tramping wildly over the underbrush.

Then—*slam!* A dull pain spread out in circles from the center of Omar's chest. He fell backward on the ground, arms and legs splayed. All at once, he was facedown, his hands joined behind his back in someone's grip.

I'm sorry, Omar," a female voice said. Not high and musical like Sophie's, but husky and matter-of-fact. "Is the vision gone?"

"Almost," Omar said as he watched the flames flicker and die around him.

"Is it safe to let go?" she asked.

"Not yet," Omar said. And so this person, whoever she was, sat on Omar's back and put him in a choke hold. "Say when, okay?"

"Okay?"

For the next few minutes Omar focused on the outline of a boot by his face until he felt like he could trust his legs again.

"Okay, now," he said, and he felt her weight lift from his body. He sat up and wiped his face.

"I'd better check you out," she said, flicking on her flashlight. Omar squinted in the light at the figure behind it. This person, whoever she was, seemed about his size, though it was hard to tell exactly because of her baggy jeans and sweatshirt. Her hood was up too, so he couldn't make out her face.

"Oh my," she said, reaching into her backpack for some ointment and bandages. Her fingers felt cool against his face.

"You'll be okay," she said. Omar must have raised his eyebrows at that line because then she laughed a little and added, "I mean, at least you're not hurt too bad."

"Thanks," Omar said, taking the light. He pointed it up so it cast a soft glow on his rescuer.

She smiled. "Rebecca," she said, holding out her hand politely. Omar took it, studying her face. She looked like a teenage version of his Aunt Lena, actually. Same square jaw, same big eyes, same frizzy, honey-colored hair.

"What?" Rebecca said.

"Uh, nothing. You look like somebody I know, that's all."

"Oh yeah? Well, you definitely don't know me."

"You're one of us, aren't you? Like me and Sophie?" Omar asked.

Rebecca leaned back and put out both hands in front of her as if she were pushing something away. "Well, like you maybe, but definitely not Sophie."

"I thought all of you were dead?" Omar said.

Rebecca laughed. "Omar, I have so much to tell you."

Omar looked at his watch. He still had twenty-five minutes to make it to the Chowder Hut. "Okay," he said to Rebecca, "but make it quick."

Omar leaned against the tree while Rebecca sat cross-legged on the ground across from him. Above, the moon had broken through the cloud cover, resolving the surrounding gray forms into silver-edged branches.

"I live in these woods too, Omar," Rebecca began, "in a shelter on the other side of the brook, and I've been watching you and Sophie." She looked up into Omar's face. "You're in deep, deep trouble."

"I know."

"I mean, like biblical trouble, Omar. Like the-devil-wants-your-soul trouble."

"Sounds like a bad story I wrote once," Omar said, smiling a little.

"Yeah, well, maybe that's why she chose you, Omar." Rebecca was not smiling. "But probably she just knew you were an easy victim—distracted parents, troubled, into vampires and crap like that."

Omar didn't have time to get offended. "You mean—Sophie's the devil?" he asked.

"Maybe not the devil, but something dark, something evil—but she's not as powerful as you might think. . . . When I knew her, she went by Lynette, but she's had a lot of names. When I met her two years ago, I was a sophomore at St. Philomena's. I'd just lost my big sister to cancer, so emotionally I was ripe for the picking. Lynette was in my skating league at the Oceans Arena."

"So what was your art?" Omar asked.

"I was a painter. Still am." Rebecca got quiet for a second. "I used to handcuff myself to the radiator when I felt a vision coming on. . . . My paintings killed a lot of people." Rebecca's voice was angry now. "When I saw the same thing happening to you, I knew now was my chance to stop her. She still believes in you— you can help me put an end to her power."

"Whoa, back up," Omar said.

"Oh, Omar!" Rebecca said. "Don't you realize that the visions are coming from her? Sophie, Lynette—whatever evil thing she is—she made you this way. You're her little work of art, don't you see? She makes you want to die from the visions, then shows up like your guardian angel. She tells you that stupid story about being so lonely and she etches your face onto her wall. Then she tells you you're finally ready and tries to turn you into a killer."

"And she's going to punish me with visions until I give in, right?" Omar was catching on now.

"Well, for a while. You have maybe another day before she loses her patience with you."

"Then what?"

"Then she'll kill you, like she killed the others."

"Wait a minute—so *you* carried out a vision?"

"Whoa—no, hold on. I didn't, Omar. Are you kidding? Actually, very few people have it in them to kill an innocent person—and I'm definitely not one of them. I pretended to die. She buried me in the ground—"

"So burying alive—that's how we die?"

"Yes, Omar, that's the only way. From dust to

dust—we take the expression to a whole new level. In any case, there I was under a foot of loose dirt, but I didn't panic. I slowed down all my muscles and my breathing. I tricked her into thinking I was dead. When she finally went away, I clawed my way out of the ground, gasping and spitting dirt everywhere."

"And the visions were gone?"

"Yes, by then she'd turned her attention to someone else. But still, I'm lonely, Omar. My family, everyone—they think I'm dead. But it's too dangerous for me to contact the people I love. If Lynette—Sophie—knows I'm living, she'll come back for me . . . Omar, I've been watching her for two years now. She's had two other victims since then, both young, lonely, and talented. Their names were Meg and Joshua—"

"Joshua Walker?" Omar interrupted.

"Yes."

"He lived in my neighborhood. I remember when he went missing. There were posters everywhere."

"Sophie got him," Rebecca explained. "And Meg too. I watched them come and go from that cabin. They must have had some hole in their lives the way you do. Sophie fills that hole. For you, it was an escape. For me, she became a new older sister.

"But Meg and Joshua—" Rebecca continued. "They're dead now, both of them. I wanted to warn them, but I had to be careful. I had to time it right to be sure they wouldn't betray me to Sophie. Meg was too afraid to walk alone in the woods. And with Joshua, I was too late. You're the first one I've been able to reach alone. Alone—in time."

Omar looked at his watch. "Jon!" he yelled. "Rebecca, I'm sorry. I have to go. I wrote a story about my friend Jon and I have to warn him before it comes true."

"Omar, listen to me," Rebecca said. "There's only one way to save Jon: go back to Sophie's. Tell her you're going to carry out a vision. That will keep her happy. She'll want details, but she's not smarter than us, Omar. You're the one with the imagination, right? Convince her, but find an excuse to put it off. Then wait for her to fall asleep. I'll be close, by waiting for you."

"Then what?"

"Don't you know, Omar? There's only one way."

Omar knew. He understood what had to be done. He just wasn't sure he'd be able to do it.

18

Omar had always been a good storyteller.

Convincing Sophie that he would kill for her—that was the tale of a lifetime. But Rebecca had been right. Once he put his imagination to use, the story was doable. It had been so long since Omar had trusted his own imagination; he'd almost forgotten that it could help him. And Rebecca was right about something else, too—Sophie wasn't as smart as she let on. Or maybe her giant ego squashed her IQ Omar found that all he had to do was compliment Sophie, tell her how right she'd been and how grateful he was.

"You saved my life, Sophie."

"Thank you for finding me."

"You're so beautiful, Sophie."

He buttered her up, and she fell for it. He made her believe that he was going to strangle Monroe tomorrow, right after dawn.

By the time Sophie put her head in Omar's lap, it was after midnight, but the light was still glaring at his portrait on the wall. For a minute, Omar watched the room's shadows cut across Sophie's face. Her skin looked gray now; he could see the loose skin under her chin, the spidery blue veins beneath her flickering eyelids.

Silently, Omar waited for Sophie to fall asleep. Eventually, her mouth went slack and her eyelids went still. He listened to her shallow breaths. Sleeping, breathing—they seemed like such normal activities for someone like her. Gently, he removed her head from his lap and placed it on a pillow. He slipped out the door and headed outside.

As soon as he was in the clearing, Omar checked his phone. He had three texts waiting for him from Jon.

Where r u?

Waiting for u

What the hell, Omar?

Jon was still alive! Omar quickly texted back, *Sorry.* One more thing he hoped he'd get a chance to explain tomorrow.

He found Rebecca in the center of the clearing. She was sitting on the giant boulder, sketching in a notebook by moonlight.

"What are you drawing?" Omar said, coming up to her.

She sprang off the rock. "Omar! God, I've been so nervous." She turned her book toward him. "See? It's you—and you don't even have an axe coming out of your head or anything."

Omar examined the drawing. His chin looked weird, and his hair was wrong, but she'd gotten his eyes perfectly. "Not bad," he said.

Rebecca grabbed back the notebook. "Just wait till I get to go to art school, Omar. I'm going to be one of the greats."

"Rebecca?" Omar said. "Why do you live like this? How come you didn't just go away? Leave Bridgewater. Find a new town, go to art school, change your identity?"

"I've thought about it. I've come close."

"But?" Omar said.

"Omar, my paintings hurt so many people. And then there were Meg and Joshua, and now you, Omar. What if I hadn't been here for you? I've stayed to do what I must. . . . Look at me, Omar." She stared him in the face. "Are you with me?"

"I think so—yes, I am."

"Because you're the one she trusts, Omar. You're on the frontline. You don't know how strong she is. Even with two of us, we have to rely on our wits, not our strength. I can help set the trap, Omar, but you have to be the bait."

Rebecca walked behind the boulder and came back carrying two shovels. She handed one to Omar. "Here." Omar wrapped his hand around its long handle. Rebecca pointed to a patch of dead ferns a few feet away. "This is where I was buried," she said, "and the others too."

Without hesitation, Omar raised his shovel and stabbed the cold, brown earth.

For hours, Rebecca and Omar dug. Shove, lift, toss. Shove, lift, toss. The repetitive motion allowed Omar to focus only on the mechanics of his body—breath, heartbeat, sweat—blocking out any other thoughts.

Omar and Rebecca spoke little—just to comment on their work and hash out the last few details of their plan. After a while, the grave became deep enough that Omar had to lower himself in to continue digging.

Omar peered at the dirt wall, just a few inches from his face. Thin, white shapes flecked its surface.

Slowly, Omar reached out to touch one. He ran his finger along its smooth surface. *Bone.*

The screaming faces of Meg, Joshua, and the others from Sophie's wall flashed in Omar's mind. He felt their screams vibrating underneath his feet, then up inside the bones of his legs and into his ribs. The sounds became muffled as dirt filled their open mouths. Omar tasted the dirt. He felt it against the roof of his mouth. Then—a damp softness against his face, behind his ears, the small of his back. The soft, rotted flesh of Sophie's victims brushed against his skin.

Omar retched. He doubled over and retched again, then again. Exhausted, he sat up and leaned against the wall. He wiped his mouth with the edge of his sleeve and waited for the voice and the urge to write it down, but only Rebecca's voice came down from above.

"You okay down there?" Rebecca's face was just a black hollow behind her hood, but Omar could make out the ragged outline of her crazy hair.

So it wasn't a vision, just his own vivid imagination.

"Yeah, I'm okay," he said.

"Do you want to switch places?"

"No, I want to do it." Omar had no idea how long he kept digging from inside the grave. When he looked up, he saw the forest floor was even with his shoulders.

"C'mon up, Omar. That's deep enough." Rebecca helped Omar out of the pit. Standing on the grave's edge, Omar checked the sky for the first time in hours; a pale blue seeped into the blackness in the east.

"Time to begin," Omar said. He felt cold suddenly. A chill shook his whole body. He wrapped his arms around himself.

"You okay, Omar?"

"Yeah, I'm okay. I'm ready," Omar said. As he headed toward Sophie's cabin, he noticed smoke curling out of her chimney.

"Where were you?" Sophie demanded as soon as Omar entered her room. She stopped suddenly when she caught sight of him. "What happened to *you?*"

"Monroe's grave," Omar said, "I'm all ready to do it, Sophie."

"Omar! I knew you wouldn't disappoint me!" Sophie held his face and kissed him softly on the lips. He held his head stiffly, forcing himself not to back away. When she pulled away, Omar noticed that her eyes were wet. "Everything's going to be okay now, Omar, you'll see," she whispered.

Omar looked down. "Okay, well, we'd better get moving." He forced himself to hold out his hand to her. Sophie took it, wide-eyed with joy, her lips parted with excitement.

Hand in hand, Omar walked with Sophie toward the clearing. "This way," Omar said. The sky was light enough now that he could clearly make out the boulder and the pit beneath it. He led Sophie to the edge of the grave and took up position behind her.

For just a second, confusion flashed over Sophie's face. "Here?" she asked. Then, suspicion. "You chose *here* for Monroe's grave, Omar?" Sophie didn't wait for Omar's answer.

"Liar!" she screamed, lunging at Omar's throat.

But a flash of metal intercepted Sophie's move. Then—*craaaaaaaack.* The bone crunching sound of the shovel hitting Sophie's skull.

Omar froze for a second, staring at Sophie's lifeless form by his feet.

"You know she's not dead, Omar—move it!" Rebecca yelled.

Omar bent down and shoved Sophie into the

pit. But even as she fell, her arms and legs started twitching.

"Start shoveling!" Rebecca screamed, as she frantically attacked the mound of dirt they had made. Omar climbed on top of the pile and started pushing with his feet. Dirt cascaded down the mound and onto Sophie's face and the long, streaked hair that pooled around her head and shoulders.

Sophie swatted at the onslaught as if it was a swarm of insects. She pointed at Omar. "Weak!" she screamed, even as the dirt rained into her open mouth. "Disappoint me!" Sophie struggled to sit up, but Omar pushed harder with his legs. A mass of dirt and stones covered her from the waist down now. Its surface heaved as her legs struggled to break free.

"You will never be free!" Sophie screamed, but it was no longer her voice. It was *that* voice—the electronic one from Omar's visions. Sophie's face looked different now too. Through the dirt, Omar could make out its greenish color.

"Coward!" Sophie's open mouth showed a row of rotten teeth. Omar caught his breath—her eyes were gone, too. In their place were empty sockets crawling with maggots. Her long, glamorous hair was replaced by a few white bristles. Sophie sat up from the waist and Omar took in the full effect of this writhing, hissing creature. It struggled and grabbed at the sides of the grave with clawlike fingers.

"Keep shoveling!" Rebecca screamed at Omar.

Omar pushed with his feet. *Hisssssss.* As the dirt hit the creature's skin, it made a sizzling noise like water dripping on a hot pan. Sophie screamed. Her back slammed back against the grave's floor. *Hisss. Hisss. Hisss.* Rebecca and Omar kept tossing as fast as they could while the creature writhed and shrieked.

Soon, Sophie was no longer visible beneath the layer of dirt, though Omar and Rebecca could still hear the shrieks. As they filled the grave, the sounds grew quieter and quieter. The surface of the dirt went from heaving to rippling until, finally, everything was quiet and still.

Rebecca and Omar dropped their shovels and collapsed on the ground. For several minutes, they stayed there, watching the sky darken, listening to their own pounding hearts.

That afternoon, Omar had a lot of explaining to do. His mom had been worried sick; Omar apologized for falling asleep at a friend's house and not calling.

"Don't worry, Mom," he said. "It will never happen again."

Later, he made up another excuse with Jon, who, like his mom, was the kind of person who was quick with forgiveness, anyway.

"But it's definitely over between you and Goth girl?" Jon asked.

"Definitely," Omar said. "Sophie's gone anyway— moved out of town, I think."

"Nice, clean break—that's the way to go," Jon replied.

The next day, reporters hounded Omar about his stories and their "supernatural" powers, but after what he'd been through, pesky journalists felt like no big deal. Plus, things were a little better at school. That afternoon, Omar emptied his savings account to buy a used laptop from Craigslist. (His mom didn't notice the difference.) The first thing Omar wrote on his new laptop was another tribute to Natasha.

A few weeks later, he read it at a special remembrance ceremony for Natasha at school. Monroe and Melissa were there that day, sitting in the audience. Monroe never did apologize, but he shook Omar's hand after Omar finished reading. And Melissa asked him to post it on Facebook, so he did.

Rebecca's reappearance made national news. The local press was camped outside her house for days, which helped take a lot of attention away from Omar. Rebecca made up some story about a kidnapper keeping her prisoner, which was kind of true. Police found Sophie's tin hut in the woods. They ID'd many of the faces on the wall. Now they were on the hunt for a killer they would never find.

In January, Rebecca enrolled in the art program at Noble College. She and Omar kept in touch, mostly through texting and e-mail. They didn't talk much about what happened in the woods. But they didn't not talk about it either. The secret lived inside both of them. They held it between them, keeping it safe in the knowledge that the visions were gone. Forever.

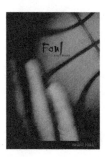